Princess School

Bobby Cinema

Order this book online at www.trafford.com
or email orders@trafford.com

Most Trafford titles are also available at major online book retailers.

Printed in the United States of America.

ISBN: 978-1-4669-3967-7 (sc)
ISBN: 978-1-4669-3968-4 (hc)
ISBN: 978-1-4669-3966-0 (e)

Library of Congress Control Number: 2012909829

Trafford rev. 06/01/2012

 www.trafford.com

North America & international
toll-free: 1 888 232 4444 (USA & Canada)
phone: 250 383 6864 ♦ fax: 812 355 4082

This book is dedicated to my niece Lakeh Chavala

Once upon a time, far off in the country of the Netherlands, a king ruled by the name of Gunther. Although his name provoked a certain foreboding notion along with his royal title, King Gunther himself was a man both wise and gentle who ruled over his people with both equal and fair treatment. Although he had ruled for more than forty years and had grown a substantial beard in his time, Gunther ruled alone. While the country remained happy in his rule, Gunther found that his only joy came from his daughter Linda, his only heir to the throne.

Often enough during the day, notions of marriage and grandchildren often found their way into King Gunther's mind, helping him to pass the time in the great throne room while he looked over the needs of his people with his Royal Advisor Walter. Today was no different as the bright visions of his daughter and his unknown son-in-law overtook his mind once more. He gazed away into his fantasies, but was soon forced back by the rustling of papers and the approach of his advisor Walter. Gunther peered

1

down at the man, a small smile touching the corner of his mouth. The small man bowed to his king.

"Hello your Majesty."

The king nodded, straightened himself in his throne, and beckoned him to approach, "What is it?"

"I just got off the phone with the last of the royal families sire, and judging by my list, the Royal Ball is already ahead of schedule."

Gunther smiled, "Excellent news Walter!" The kings' thoughts shifted to his daughter, and his smile quickly faded. "I'm not so certain how Linda will take the news though, what are your thoughts?"

Walter found himself quickly looking at the floor. "Hard to say your Majesty. The princess is not exactly keen on the idea of this royal function. She loathes these things. It's always about appearances, prestige, and mingling properly. These particular elements of society are sometimes elusive to your daughter."

Gunther shifted himself in his seat once more. "You think I don't know that? My daughter will be turning eighteen this coming week, already a young woman! My only wish for this ball is to help her take a proper step towards functioning as a woman of royalty should . . ."

Walter looked up from the floor, a slight grin passing over his face. He waited for the rest of Gunther's' thoughts to come out.

". . . Annnd, of course finding a proper suitor who is worthy to marry the princess someday."

Walter smiled and nodded in agreement. "Right you are sire."

Gunther stood, stretched, and clasped Walter on the shoulder. They walked the long throne room, Walter listening as the king continued.

"Yes Walter, I worry about her. I know she is thinking about going to college soon, but she needs the right man with royal blood at her side when she goes off to college. That way, once she graduates from school, she will be ready to take over the throne with her new husband."

Walter nodded. "That's one of the many reasons why she hates these parties sire. You're always trying to set her up with one of the princes or dukes noble blood."

Gunther cast a quick glance at his advisor as they continued to walk. Silence remained heavy for a short time and soon the king found himself curling his beard in his fingers. Walter smiled and looked down, knowing that the king's actions were a sure tell of being both nervous and anxious. At last the king spoke, "I know she wants to marry for love Walter, and I will respect her wishes. Just so, we will arrange this event to be open to everyone in the country."

Walter's gaze met the floor again at the news. The king shook him and grinned heartedly down at his advisor. "Walter, I want you to send out the invitations to everybody in this country to spread the word."

Walter nodded, "Yes, your highness."

"And remember Walter, Linda needs to a find a potential suitor, and if you mess this up, you'll be cleaning the royal stables all month. If you do really well with this party, I will offer you a great reward. Now . . . what did I just say?"

Walter quickly looked up, "Don't mess this up?"

Gunther shook him again, grinning all the more. "Exactly! Linda will be in charge of this ball, but she won't know the ropes. Just so, I will arrange for her to go to a Princess School for a week. This will help teach her the proper function of these events."

Walter raised an eyebrow towards his king's statement. "But sire, we don't have a Princess School."

"We do now," Gunther declared. "It will be here. You will be teaching these young princes and princesses everything to do for this royal ball before they are brought to society."

Walter suddenly felt himself growing pale and weak under this new request. Managing one royal daughter was hard enough at times, but managing multiple princes and princesses sounded like a royal nightmare. Gunther reached into this jacket pocket and handed a list to Walter. The king continued to talk as Walter read the list.

"The Royal Ball is in two weeks. We have a week to get everything ready. This list marks the princes and princesses that will attend the school. You're going to give them the lessons about attending the ball. Mail out the invitations to those on the list promptly, we need to get started."

Walter pocketed the list. "Don't worry sire, I will get everything ready."

"Good, now go find Linda and tell her what's going on."

Walter bowed out from underneath his king's grip on his shoulder and made for a hasty exit from the throne room.

"Walter . . . . remember . . ."

Walter turned to find his king pointing his royal finger back at him. Walter nodded, "Don't mess this up . . . yes sire."

Gunther nodded at his answer and continued to walk the room as Walter quickly ushered himself out. The hallways were silent as he continued to move room to room, down one hallway and on to the next. He soon found himself to the private rooms of the royal estate. As he came to Linda's room, he could hear the voices of one of Linda's favorite television programs heard in the room.

"Gossip Girl", he thought as turned the doorknob. He smiled to himself, admiring the young princess because for all her royal baggage that she inherited, young Linda still managed to keep the life of a normal teenage girl. Walter always liked that about her, her ability to remain normal without all the pomp that can get to a young girl's head, especially a young girl of royalty.

He opened the door to find Linda sprawled out on her couch, facing the TV just as he predicted. She smiled at him as he entered.

"Hello Walter."

Walter bowed slightly, "Hello young miss. I have a message from your father."

Linda hit the mute button on the controls. "What is it?"

"Your father needs to see you in the throne room right away. There is something he wants to talk to you about."

The young girl cringed slightly at Walter's words, *"Oh man, I think he's mad that he found my application to U.S.C. I don't want to go to his alma mater!"* Her thoughts break off to the sound of Walter clapping.

"Chop chop your majesty! Your father needs to see you right away."

Linda sighed as she reached up with the remote and turned the TV off. They quickly made their way back to the throne room to find the king still pacing and curling his beard in his fingers. At the sight of his young daughter he clapped his hands behind his back, smiling down at this daughter as she approached. Linda could see her father was nervous about something and although she didn't like the situation one bit, she also didn't like to see her father nervous or upset. She quickly hugged him to help ease his tension.

"Hello father, Walter told me you wanted to see me? What's the word?"

The king looked at her curiously. "Um . . . well honey, next week will be your eighteenth birthday. You'll be going to a college after that. We are throwing a royal ball as your farewell banquet before you go out into the world."

Linda's shoulders slumped at her father's words. "Another royal ball? Dad . . . for just once, can I please have a nice quiet evening instead of these formals and banquets that we have to throw every year?"

Linda's father smiled at her reaction. "You are the future Queen of the Netherlands. I will need someone to run the country. I won't be around forever you know."

Linda turned away from her father. "So you need me to run the country so I can throw parties like this?"

"Exactly my dear. You will be addressing the nation and throwing premieres and galleries. I need to make sure you're in line after you graduate college and can work with our government and me to keep our country going."

"I get it dad, but do I really need another royal ball for my eighteenth birthday?"

"Yes! This will be our farewell party to this country before you head off to see the world, one of which you have never seen before!"

Linda nodded and rolled her eyes. "Okay dad, I understand."

Linda's father hugged her from behind, his beard messing her hair. "Excellent! You will be in charge of throwing your own royal ball."

Linda turned to face her father, her expression changing from pure gloom to utter bewilderment. "What do you mean, I'll be in charge? What do I know about running my own royal ball?"

Walter shuffled forward clearing his throat. "That's where I come in, for a week we're opening a school where we teach young prince and princesses how to prepare royal balls and functions like this."

King Gunther proudly puffed out his chest at Walter's statement. "We're calling it *Princess School.*"

Linda stared blankly back at the two men. Both Walter and Gunther exchanged glances at one another, and once more Gunther began twirling his beard. Walter could sense the awkwardness to continue to rise so he pressed forward.

"We're going to pick five princes and princesses to attend this school and teach them to prepare for a royal ball. Your father's only wish is for this school to help prepare all of you for society, when you are ready for your royal duties."

Linda scoffed at Walter's statement and looked down, *Making them the next royal snobs.* She mumbled.

Gunther spoke, "I have already selected the five princes and princesses who will attend this school. Walter will be sending the invitations out in a few hours, so once they have all arrived we will start the school and you will begin your training."

Linda's face began to turn red. "Suppose I go along with this princess school, who is going to teach this class?"

"I am." Replied Walter.

Linda looked at Walter from the corner of her eye with enough time to catch a quick wink from her advisor. She smiled, thinking of Walter as her teacher.

"In that case, I'm in." Said Linda.

Gunther's voice boomed throughout the room at Linda's answer. He grabbed a hold of both of them and hugged them close. He smiled and looked down at his daughter.

"I knew you would come around! Your mother would be so pleased with what you're doing."

Linda smiled up at her father. "I know it was her dream for me to learn the rules of court and society and also for me to go to Oxford University where you both attended. But honestly dad, is going to Oxford really all that necessary?"

"Yes!" Gunther boasted, "It taught me and your mother important things about life and society. It will help you make you a woman your mother would be proud of. And who knows? Maybe one of the princes in our little school will be engaged to you someday!"

I was afraid you would say that. Linda thought. "Yeah maybe dad, who knows?"

Gunther turned back to Walter who had slipped from the king's grasp and now stood, watching silently.

"We better get started Walter. Make out the invitations to the five prince and princesses who are being invited to the ball," He turned back to Linda, "Honey, if you're finishing up your college application to Oxford, let me know. Walter will pick up your application and that's it. You will be a shoe-in for admittance, don't worry about that."

Linda followed Walter's cue and uncurled herself from her father's arm.

"Okay. I better head back to my room then and finish the application. I'll let Walter know when I'm done."

Linda's father smiled and nodded, his hand ushering her away. She took her time walking back to her room, knowing that all that was said in the throne room was still slowly settling in her mind. Her mind clicked back on once she heard the click of her doorknob opening to her room. She needed someone ... ANYONE to talk to, and while she would normally welcome to the company of Walter for a friendly chat, given the circumstances, she decided against it. Without thinking, she rushed to her computer and clicked on to her chat screen. Most of her friends' statuses read OFFLINE, but she smiled when she saw the green ONLINE icon of her friend Billy shining back at her. Billy had been Linda's chat partner and pen pal for over a year now and had always been there for her on both her best and worst days. Although neither had ever met in life, Linda felt a strong connection to Billy. They both lived completely different lives, one of royalty, the other of common every day individuals. And not only was there the gap of society between them, but a very large ocean as well. Billy lived in California, making the friendship all more difficult, but neither of them seemed to mind. And although Billy had never known of Linda's background, both Linda and Billy felt that they truly knew each other for whom they really were.

Linda clicked on Billy's icon and a small chat box popped up on her desktop. She began typing:

> Linda: Hi Billy! Another stressful day today, reaaaaaally wish you were here to talk about it in person. Do you think we will meet up at some point?
> Billy: I would definitely like to! What's bugging you?
> Linda: Well, I'm about to go in college in the near future. I have to mail my application in today

and they'll let me know in about a week or so
if I got in.

Billy: Awesome! Are you applying to U.S.C? You
always talk about living a normal life like a
regular person . . . why is that so important
anyways?

Linda: I just want to go to a college where nobody
knows me and likes me for who I am. Not just
what I can offer to society or something.

Billy: Welcome to my world! In high school I was
labeled as an outsider. Maybe this will be a
first to where I can have a clean slate and just
be . . . me. You know?

Linda smiled at Billy's response and continued to type.

Linda: Outsider means total geek Billy. :-P

Billy: You betcha! If you get into U.S.C., maybe I'll
see you there. I applied there specifically to the
school of cinema and got my letter yesterday.
I GOT IN!!!

Linda slumped back into her chair for a moment. She was
happy for Billy, but still incredibly envious. Billy was a terrific
friend, but he was also her only link to anything of the outside
world. The stories he told her sounded amazing and exciting to
her and above all else for Linda, Billy sounded free. Free in ways
that she had never known and constantly wondered if she ever
would. The screen continued to stare back at her. Finally, she put
keys to fingers and continued.

Linda: Sound amazing, congratulations.

Billy: Someday, I am going to be like my hero, Josh Schwartz.

Linda: Josh Schwartz . . . the youngest producer who created the O.C., Gossip Girl and Chuck!?

Billy: Top marks! That's him!

Linda: That's awesome! You already have a major you want to focus on too! Truth be known, my father wants me to pick finance and economics as my major because it's for the family business. After I graduate, I'm supposed to join him and pick up my own part of the business.

Billy: That must suck.

Linda: Well yeah, but I have no choice. Since I'm the only heir to the thro . . . . business.

Billy: So . . . . if finance and economics isn't your major what is?

Linda: I have no idea, but I always wanted to major in government and go to law school someday where I can make a difference.

Billy: Then go for it! Maybe you should tell your dad that?

Linda: I think he would understand that I want to major in government and go to law school. He won't understand that I want to go to U.S.C. because he wants me to go to Oxford.

Billy: . . . . what? Oxford!? Why?

Linda: Because he went to school there. So did my grandfather and mother. It's a "family tradition" that I go there.

11

> Billy: One thing I can tell you, traditions only stand the chance that they will be broken someday.

Linda leaned forward and re-read Billy's words. *He's right!* She thought to herself. Again, Billy continued to amaze her.

> Linda: You're right Billy, they are meant to be broken, but I don't want to hurt my father. My mother died last year, and it was her request to him that I carry on the tradition and go to Oxford.
>
> Billy: Did your mom REALLY want you to go to Oxford, or to follow your heart?
>
> Linda: Surprisingly, she didn't say that before she died. Most moms do right? She only said that to my father; she didn't want to hurt his feelings. I guess I'm doing the same thing. Going to Oxford would just make him happy.
>
> Billy: Then I would back off. It's your choice, not your dad's. YOURS!
>
> Linda: After I get my letter, I will let you know if I get in or not. I need to keep my options open.
>
> Billy: That's the spirit! ☺
>
> Linda: I wish we could meet sometime before we head off to college. If I get into U.S.C., I would most likely spend my time wandering the halls looking for you.
>
> Billy: Don't sweat it, here's my address: Billy Malcolm, 1236 Lincoln Boulevard, Anaheim CA, 92801. Just write me a letter and mail

it to me and let me know if you want to meet
anytime or any place before we head off to
college.

Linda: Fair enough. I will let you know tomorrow.
I best jump off for now and get my application
done. Thanks, bye Billy.

Billy: Bye Linda, and see ya!

Billy's status disappeared from Linda's screen and she was left on her own again. She glanced at some of the final comments, found his address, and copied and pasted it to a document so she could have it on hand. She saved one on her computer, and quickly jotted it down on a piece of paper on her desk for a backup copy. Her eyes went from the address to the two yellow envelopes that looked up at her. One letter was her application to Oxford, the other to U.S.C. She held both of them in her hands, almost weighing them against each other in hopes their worth would come through with the weight. Unfortunately, both were pretty even. A loud buzz from her intercom pulled her away from the applications and she clicked the green button.

"Yes?"

"Hi Linda, are you done filling out your college application yet?"

Walter's voice made her smile. He had a nice subtle way of being direct with her without coming off cross or stern. She looked at the application to U.S.C. again. Walter's voice chimed in again.

"I'm finished with printing the invitations to the princes and princesses. If you're finished with the application, put it in a yellow envelope so I can mail it out with the rest. Oh! And another thing, Prince Richard who was to be enrolled in the school can't make it. He has the measles. He can make it to the ball but not the school. I don't suppose you know of any other prince, duke, lord, or ambassador's son that can replace him do you? I um . . . . I just want to do this right."

Linda's eyes went wide and she slammed her hand back down on the green button.

"Yes! I have his address here!

"Who is it?" Walter asked.

Linda's hands were shaking under the excitement. She fumbled around underneath the letters to find the address.

"His name is Prince William Malcolm, 1236 Lincoln Boulevard, Anaheim, CA 92801, that's where he is."

"Hmm . . . interesting address your highness. The address is in the United States? Why is the prince living in that area?"

"It's one of the prince's summer homes," she replied. "He lives in the embassy in L.A. and spends the summer in America."

The intercom crackled as she heard Walter hit the button again.

"What is Prince William the prince OF exactly?"

"He's . . . umm . . . the prince of the Ukraine. His uncle is the king of Belgium."

A long pause could be heard on Walter's end. She had a bad feeling she was blowing any chance of seeing Billy, especially with the stretch she was giving Walter. She hated to lie to Walter, he was a terrific friend of hers, but she couldn't risk telling him the truth and having her father forbid Billy coming to see her.

"King of Belgium . . . King Gustavo is William's uncle?"

"That's right, he's his nephew like I said. His father is Gustavo's brother."

"Very good your highness. I will send him an invitation and make sure that the limo and jet will pick him up and bring him to the castle."

Linda practically beamed at Walter's answer.

"Thank you Walter."

"You're welcome miss."

Linda let go of the intercom button and immediately set to filling out her application to U.S.C. Her mind was made up, Billy was right. She found Walter in his office, seeing to the final letters to be mailed. She greeted him, grinning from ear to ear. She smiled up at her from behind his desk and quickly set himself back to work. He reached up with an empty hand as he was signing off on a post, and Linda quickly placed the letters in his hand.

"Thank you your highness."

"You're welcome sir." She replied. She did a quick curtsey and left Walter bustling about with his work. He smiled as she left, and didn't bother to look as he stuffed her letters in with the rest of the mail. Soon enough, the letters were sent out through mail services in the west end of the castle, and soon enough, out to greet the guests for Princess School.

.   .   .   .

The sun shined brightly on the back of Billy's bike as he raced home from school. The mid-afternoon heat was too hot and humid to his liking, and sweat rolled down his face as he made one last turn into his driveway. He jumped from the bike, letting it crash into the grass and dove for the cool comforts of his air-conditioned home. He found his usual spot on the couch and landed with a soft *thud*. He flipped on the television, and did his quick afternoon ritual of flipping through channel after channel finding nothing interesting on. He left it on the afternoon show *Hollywood Buzz* and while the reporter went on about the latest action film, Billy flipped through the mail. He found two letters addressed to him, one being a packet containing a large amount of information to U.S.C.

He quickly tore open the package, finding a lot of the usual *What it means to be a U.S.C. student*, as well as, *Getting you started* nonsense. He quickly skimmed the material, knowing that he would be going all over it again when he went for his freshman seminar class. Most of the information was useful and interesting, but the thought of the second letter took him away from U.S.C. and on to the strange letter addressed to: *Prince William Malcolm*. He tore open the envelope, finding a brightly colored card addressed to him, displaying a brief message.

To Prince William Malcolm,

Sir, the honor of your presence is requested for the royal function of Princess School in honor of Princess Linda, and her upcoming eighteenth birthday. The proceedings are to take place in two days time, a limousine will arrive promptly at five o'clock a.m. to escort you to the airport, where you will take a private jet to Princess Linda's home in the Netherlands. This high honor is to assist future rulers of our world's finest countries in matters of state, courtly behavior, and all manners of appearance, appreciation, and applying oneself to their country. We look forward to being in your presence shortly.

Highest regards,

King Gunther, Princess Linda, and royal staff

Billy turned the card over and over again, trying to find a hidden message or joke to his strange invitation but found none. He sat confused by the message, but soon relaxed thinking of his friend Jimmy. They had been best friends since grade school, and ever since their first day of meeting, Jimmy was constantly trying to improve his practical jokes on Billy. They grew larger and larger as the years passed, and Billy smiled to himself thinking his friend had finally outdone himself. He grinned and nodded, allowing himself to accept Jimmy's terms, knowing that is was most likely some last-minute joke that his friend was trying to pull before they parted ways for college. *All right Jimmy, one last show for old time's sake.*

He ran upstairs and packed a quick bag of clothes for a few days, smiling as he zipped the bag shut. That evening, while eating with his parents, he told them about the card and the limo, telling them to just go along with it. He smiled knowing that he would have to think of something even bigger to get back at his friend. He slept lightly, and when his alarm went off at 4:30 the following morning, Billy made a mad dash for his clothes and was waiting outside one the curb in a manner of minutes. He looked down the street and spotted the headlights of the limo as it rounded the corner. He stood and watched as the car pulled to a stop, his grinning reflection looking back at him from the darkened window. The chauffer stepped out, bowing slightly as he rounded the car.

"Morning!" Said Billy. The driver stopped and looked at Billy for a moment, eyeing him a bit suspiciously.

"Good morning sir, are you ready to go? We must make your flight in time for the commencement."

Billy smiled and nodded, *Man . . . Jimmy sure did pull out all the stops on this one.* He straightened himself, allowing for a ridiculous imitation of a prince to come to him, and nodded once more. "Yes my good man, please take me promptly to the airport, we must make haste if we are to arrive on schedule." The last word schedule came out sounding more like *shhedule,* thinking of all the times he watched movies where royalty pronounced it so. The driver gave Billy an odd look but quickly dismissed his manner.

"Yes sir, right away sir." He opened the back door and took his duffle bag. Once Billy sat down the driver quickly closed the door and popped his bag in the trunk. The drive didn't take long, and soon he found himself at Anaheim airport, on one of the smaller, independent runways looking up at a private jet. He walked up the stairs to the door, keeping his regal appearance up as the pilot greeted him. The pilot extended his hand, and while Billy went to shake it, the pilot replied curtly, "Invitation sir." Billy handed him his invitation, a bit crumpled from his back pocket, and the pilot examined it closely. He soon pocketed the paper and stepped aside to allow Billy to enter the plane.

As he sat, listening the plane power up, the slow *hummmm* of the engines slowly relaxed Billy. He slumped down in his leather seat. *Ok Jimmy, where are you? This is a bit much.* His brow furrowed as he looked over his shoulder waiting for his friend to pop out of some hidden door, but the only person he found walking towards him was the stewardess.

"Umm, excuse me miss?"

The young woman looked down at Billy, smiling. "Yes my lord? How can I help you?"

"Well . . . I umm . . . . where is the jet going?"

The lady looked at him then as if he were trying to pull a joke on her. She smiled and shook her head. "Well, our destination is Amsterdam of course, to King Gunther's castle."

Billy nodded. "Right, right. That's in the Netherlands right?"

"Of course it is sir." Replied the woman.

Billy nodded once more, slumping down into his seat again. "I don't suppose you have any Diet Coke do you?" The stewardess smiled. "Of course we do sir." Billy held up his fingers. "Can I get two cans please?" The stewardess smiled and nodded and walked to the back of the plane. As he waited, Billy could feel his eyes starting to droop slightly. All of the excitement of the morning had caught up with him, and so had his apparent lack of sleep from the night before. The young lady came back and poured one of the cans into a cup. As Billy listened to the soft *hiss* of the soda, he felt sleep slowly taking back a hold of him. As he drifted off, he swore he could feel the wheels beneath him roll out onto the strip, and the engines grow louder and louder. He felt a slight rush come to his stomach as he felt the ground give way, and before passing out completely, he thought to himself, *Jimmy . . . you've outdone yourself again. Well-played sir.*

.　.　.　.

Billy passed in and out of dreams. He thought of castles, and royal balls, and fancy suits. The dreams were a swirl of colors, music, and from what he could tell, and overall good time. Before the dream had finished though, he could hear the voice of the nice flight attendant waking him.

"Sir, we have arrived. Welcome to the Netherlands, your limo is waiting for you."

Billy smiled and thanked the attendant. He looked over at his cup holder to find the Diet Coke untouched from the night before. He checked his watch to see that he had slept away the entire day. He quickly grabbed his bag and made for the door. He looked down at the bottom of the ramp to find the same limo driver waiting for him, the limo already pointed towards the road.

"Hi again. Umm, which airport are we at here? Are we still in Anaheim?"

The driver rolled his eyes slightly. "No sir, we have arrived at our destination in the Netherlands, I am to escort you to the castle where his Majesty's staff are waiting."

Billy suddenly felt pale, and let his bag fall from his shoulder. "Then this . . . this is all . . . real then?" The driver couldn't take anymore of Billy's ridiculous questions. He sighed heavily and took his bag to the car.

"I am sure his Grace will enjoy your ever-so clever notions of comedy sir." He opened the back door, allowing Billy to crawl inside. Within moments, the car had left the runway, and Billy soon found himself driving down the main strip of Amsterdam on his way to the castle. *This is all real . . . unbelievable!* Billy watched out the window as the foreign land greeted, and passed him by. Within an hour they were out of the city, and making their way over the rich green landscape. *Ok, ok, no need to panic Billy, once we get to the castle, just explain everything and get your butt back on the plane for home.* He continued to think of what or even, *how* he was going to explain himself to his parents, let alone the King of the Netherlands. He looked down to his hands growing pale and feeling clammy. He felt the limo turn a corner, and as he looked up, he managed to catch a glimpse of the castle before him.

The castle itself was immense, towering above the tree line like a huge stone sentinel in the middle of the woods. The lawns and surrounding area reflected both the regal and noble natures of its occupants and as the limo rounded the drive to the front doors, Billy sat awestruck, taking in deep breaths in hopes that he wouldn't pass out or worse. The driver opened his door and Billy staggered out of the backseat, shouldering his pack. He made his way to the large front doors of the main hall, the staff already lined up and waiting for his arrival. An older man smiled and bowed quickly escorted Billy to the throne room.

"Please wait here for a moment sir, Walter will be with your shortly." The man turned to leave, but Billy stopped him. "Who is Walter?" The butler looked back over his shoulder as he left. "He is King Gunther's royal advisor sir." The older gentleman quickly closed the doors behind him, and as Billy shifted his gaze around the room, he noticed he wasn't alone. In various other areas in the room were other people that were roughly Billy's age. They paid no attention to him, merely looked over their shoulders, or passed a quick leering gaze in his direction, but no one introduced themselves. Some talked amongst one another, or, studied the paintings on the wall. Billy continued to stand exactly where he was left, his wrinkled clothes and bag made him feel more like a beggar in comparison to the other individuals in room. *God, I want to go home!* Billy thought. No sooner had he finished his wish, the double doors opened again and a man and a young woman entered the room.

Walter and Linda surveyed the room and watched as the other princes and princesses slowly made their way towards them. Before they were reached, Walter noticed the strange disheveled looking boy and walked towards him briskly. Billy took a step back and pawed at his bag on his shoulder. Walter opened what Billy recognized as his invitation, and inspected it and then looked up at the young guest. Billy looked over Walter's shoulder to the young woman standing behind him. Her face had changed to a bright red, and he constantly looked from the floor, to Billy, then back down again.

"So you are Prince William Malcolm then I take it?" Walter asked.

Billy grabbed for his bag again and shifted slightly. "Well sir, I . . ."

"I take it your flight was comfortable? Awfully long way to travel in such short of time. My apologies for the last minute request."

Billy felt weak for a moment. "Oh! No seriously, no problem. But, I think . . ."

"You are here," Walter interjected, "to learn the finer points of what it means to be a prince young Master Malcolm. As I have already discussed with the other members of royalty here, you will be taught on the finer qualities of nobility. Not only that, but you will also have to be taught in five different areas of planning royal function."

Billy managed to blink of his eyes. "Function?" Walter sighed slightly and continued.

"Yes, Master Malcolm. Functions such as royal balls, charities, fundraisers and the like. But before we get started, and you are shown to your respected rooms, let me introduce you all in full."

The other princes and princesses had gathered into standing order as Billy was escorted to their ranks. He managed to slink his way in between two others, but dared not look up as he could feel their eyes on him, judging him, looking down on him. *I've got to get out of here!* Billy screamed in his mind. Yet, he still managed to look towards the young woman standing next to Walter. She smiled at him, expressing a notice that suggested to Billy that she knew him, although he knew that to be ridiculous. Walter stood in front of the guests as he continued his speech.

"Good afternoon my lords and ladies of the court. On behalf of his Majesty King Gunther, Princess Linda, myself, and the royal staff, I would like to thank you all for attending this academy. As I have discussed with all of you already, we will be focusing on the finer points of your royal positions, as well as discussing plans and details for managing charities, fundraisers, and the like. As a "test run" so to speak, you will all be taking part in the plans and preparations of the royal ball that is to commence a week from now on behalf of Princess Linda's 18th birthday. This will be Linda's farewell party before she heads off to college, but this party is also for all of you, for you all will soon be parting for college and for what the real world has to offer. Before I announce the five areas that we are going to teach here, I'm going to give role call to make sure everyone is here."

Walter pulled a list from his jacket, unfolded it, and held it out in front: "Princess Jeannette, daughter of King Antonio and Queen Sophia of Italy." A young woman in front of Billy curtseyed slightly at her announcement. Walter continued. "Princess Anna, daughter of King Gunner and Queen Katherine of Belgium, Princess Jessica, daughter of King Jenga of Romania, Princess Diane, daughter of King Edward and Queen Lana of Monaco, Prince Edward, son of King Rutger and Queen Lisa, and also his sister, Princess Anna." The two individuals next to Billy nodded and curtseyed. "Prince Anthony, son of King Alexander and Queen Holly of Greece. Prince Oliver, son of King Musgrave and Queen Laura of Switzerland. And last, but certainly not least, Prince William Malcolm, nephew to King Gustavo of the Ukraine."

Billy managed to raise his hand to say hi, but quickly put his hand down again as Walter continued. "Now, the five areas we will teach. First will be decorations; we will teach you about how to discuss, plan, and organize with our decorating committee to figure out what would be appropriate to decorate the ballroom. Second will be food, where we will discuss what will be acceptable as food to be prepared for the ball. Third shall be invitations, fourth will be posture, as I'm sure you all know is one of the highlights in maintaining a positive image when out in public. The final area will be in entertainment, where we will discuss what measures should be taken when entertaining the guests at a ball. At the end of the week, I will look at your results from the week of training and decide which shall be the more engaging of the ideas. The winner will be put in charge alongside Princess Linda in decorating for the ball. And like all ceremonies, when the ball has finished for the evening, we will then crown the winners of Princess School. Decoration planning will start promptly at 8 a.m. tomorrow morning, I bid you all a very good night, your ushers will show you to your respected rooms."

Billy looked over his shoulder to see two men enter pulling trolleys will luggage on them. They stopped in front of the guests, and Walter continued. "My ladies will follow Pierre here," he pointed to the man on his left. "And my lords will follow Alfred. Now, one of you young ladies will have to share a room with Princess Linda," Walter turned towards her. "My lady Linda, which would you prefer?"

Linda took a moment, but finally pointed towards who Billy remembered as Jessica. "I will take Princess Jessica in my wing Walter." Said Linda. Walter nodded, "Very good my lady." Linda stepped forward and Walter stepped back a step as she spoke. "Walter, our guests will need as much accommodation as we can provide, but we are short on space with so many here. Since William is the last to arrive, we shall have to have his quarters next to mine," She turned to look at Billy. "Please forgive me William on this matter, I hope this will not upset you during your stay."

The others turned to look at Billy, but all he could manage was a slight high-pitched laugh. He put his hands up. "I'm good with whatever you can provide . . . my lady." He looked around to see the others scoffing at his remark, and he quickly looked down again. Walter nodded to the ushers and soon Billy and the others were pushed along their way towards their respected rooms. As Billy walked towards his room, he felt a hand on his shoulder. He turned to see Linda looking at him.

"Billy, there is something I need to talk with you about."

Billy looked at her in surprise. "How did you know I went by Billy?" Linda quickly dismissed the question. "I'll be by to see you in a moment, just let me get Jessica settled."

Billy nodded, and Linda disappeared into the next room. He was quickly ushered into his room where he found all the latest and best that life could provide for a guy at his age: TV, computer with wi-fi, hundreds of channels, DVD players, large closets, and the finest bed and sofas that only royalty could afford. He dropped his bag on the floor and heard the door close behind him. He turned to see Linda standing in front of him. She smiled awkwardly at him.

"I know this is probably all quite a shock to you Billy, but I actually know you."

Billy stared blankly back at her. "I don't think you do miss, and I think there has been a mistake here." Linda crossed the room and now stood in front of him.

"There's no mistake, you see, I'm your pen pal . . . . from the chat room."

Billy's heart felt like it was about to explode. He suddenly felt light-headed and sat down quickly.

"You're Linda!? From the chat room!?"

"Yes."

"Linda, you realize I'm NOT royalty. I live in the middle of suburbia city in Anaheim! What are you thinking!?"

"I know that!" Exclaimed Linda. "I know all about you remember? I just wanted to meet you in person before I left for school. THAT's why you got the invitation. I addressed you as a prince to convince my father and Walter. We've been friends long enough online, I just felt that we should finally meet, even if it's only for a short time. I'm sorry if I upset you."

Billy stood and looked at Linda. "I'm not upset . . . well . . . not NOW anyways. I can understand why you would want to meet, and I'm glad we have. But Linda, I'm thinking royalty would look down on a commoner like me. I'm not like anyone here."

"I like you for who you are Billy," Linda replied. "And if my father can't understand that, I will renounce my throne and hand over my crown, and he can find someone else to run the

Netherlands. I just wanted this one chance to meet you before we go to college."

"Which college are you going to?" Asked Billy.

"I want to go to U.S.C."

"Then you should go Linda! That's where I got accepted to yesterday! If we're going to the same place, we could see each other there."

Linda shied away from him. "I haven't received my acceptance letter yet. I have no idea whether I got in or not. I won't hear from them for a week."

Billy looked at her quizzically. "Why's that?"

"My father and the rest of my family went to Oxford University. He expects me to go there and follow in his and my mother's footsteps. But Billy, I want to follow my own path, not theirs."

"So what would happen if you just told him that? That you wanted to go to U.S.C. instead of Oxford?"

Linda shook her head. "I would hurt him greater than I ever have. He would be incredibly disappointed if I didn't go to Oxford. But on the other hand, he has to let me go sooner or later Billy. I just don't know what to do."

Billy ushered her towards the couch and they both sat.

"Ok Linda, that's one problem, and we can work that out, I'm sure of it. But the other issue at hand is with this Princess School. What am I going to do!? Don't you think we should tell Walter, or someone before this gets out of hand?"

"If you tell Walter, he will probably just send you home, and I will never get a chance to see you again. Even if I don't get into U.S.C., we should at least have this one chance of knowing and being with each other before we go to different colleges."

Billy smiled as Linda spoke. He could feel himself relax more, and felt himself warming up inside while he talked with her. After a moment, he grabbed a hold of Linda's hand and smiled.

"Alright then. I'll go along with it Linda. You're right, even if we have to part ways in a week, at least we have the week."

Linda smiled up at him, and could feel tears started to well up behind her eyes.

"Thank you Billy. Truly, I can't tell you that enough. Thank you for coming here. I best get back to Jessica before rumors start flying."

Billy walked her to the door and opened it for her. She smiled once more at him as she left. She turned back to him. "Remember, decorations start at 8."

"I'll be sure to be there, goodnight Linda." He closed the door and leaned up against it, listening to her footsteps move across the hall to her room. Once he heard the door shut, he sighed heavily. *I love you,* was all he could manage to say and think the rest of the evening. He rifled through his bag and tried to straighten his clothes as best as he could. He was bound and determined not to screw anything up this week. Even if he couldn't be with Linda, he was going to try to his hardest to be the best at Princess School. He would give them a show like they had never seen before.

. . . .

By the time his alarm went off the following morning, Billy was still trying to decide if he was awake, or still in the dream that he had on plane. Seeing how he remembered the plane however, and that his bedroom had changed slightly from his home in Anaheim, he accepted that it was no dream. Seeing that it was

7:30 already, he lunged out of bed and quickly got ready. He was soon out of his room, running down the hallway in frantic search for the dining room. He met a maid on the stairway and she told him, "down the stairs here and to your right." Billy had to laugh at himself. Back home, being tardy multiple times could land you in detention. He could only imagine what it would mean if he showed up late at a royal convention.

The room was right where the maid had said, and Billy bolted into the room. He slammed into a table, knocking off a vase of flowers that stood on its edge. The shattering vase echoed through the large room and Billy soon found himself eye-to-eye with Walter.

"I'm sorry sir." Replied Billy.

Walter shook his head. "It's all right sir, no need to trouble yourself with that. Pierre!" Walter beckoned for the nearby usher.

"I'll get a broom Walter." Said Pierre as he shuffled by. Billy looked around the room to see the others laughing under their breath at the display. Linda stood at the head of the table.

"I'll help you with that Pierre. It's my fault, and my responsibility, I'm the one that did it after all."

The usher smiled at Billy. "I'd appreciate that sir, most kind of you."

After the mess was broomed away, Walter began to explain the layout of the day.

"Lords and ladies, today we will discuss the preparations that need to be made in terms of decorating. These things will encompass the largest of items, to the smallest. For instance, the right streamers, napkins, and centerpieces. You need the right decorations for the occasion, so I am curious to know what your thoughts are on the matter." He turned towards Princess Diane. "My lady, what napkin design would you pick for the royal ball?"

The young girl stood and cleared her throat. "Golden flowers with blue stripes."

"Excellent choice lady. Prince Antonio, what are your thoughts on streamers?"

The young man named Antonio stood. "White stripes and black trimmings in the streamers sir."

Walter thought about his answer for a moment. "Wrong young sir. White trimmings and blue stripes would be more appropriate I feel. Remember, this is about making great first impressions to your guests." Walter's gaze now shifted to Billy, who had made his way to the table. "William, if you were making a good first impression for the ball, what plates would you choose?"

Billy stared blankly back at Walter. The other princes and princesses grew silent as they waited Billy's reply. "Umm, well sir . . . I suppose I would go with . . ." He looked at Linda whose eyes had grown wide, anxious for his answer. "I would go with a gorgeous silver and gold flower inlay, designed within a leaf pattern."

Walter smiled then at the response Billy gave. "You have done your homework William, excellent choice. If you have a long way to go yet, but keep giving answers like that, and I'm sure you'll graduate this course with top marks."

Billy sat down and looked around. The others were smiling and nodding in his direction, especially Linda, who beamed at the head of the table. Walter moved next to her.

"Remember students, you will be picking up your decorations and designing your own centerpiece when you get back to the castle. You can use one of the rooms in the castle to decorate your piece, and, you may choose a decorating partner. I will be the judge of the decorations. If I pick you, it will be used in the ball. The overall winner of this week's judging will ALSO receive a scholarship in a 100,000 of your selected school's currency. The limousines will be here within the hour, so pick your partner and I'll call you when we are ready to leave."

The students talked amongst themselves, eating, and walking about the room. Billy could see people starting to pair up, so he went about the room asking if anyone would be interested. After enough "no's" and "sorry's" he began to feel sick that he might not find anyone. He soon felt a familiar hand on his shoulder and turned to find Linda looking up at him. Billy smiled at her.

"I don't suppose you would want to team up?"

Linda smiled and turned away. "Nah . . ."

Billy looked away for a moment, his confidence starting hang even lower. Linda quickly spun around. "Of COURSE I'll be your partner!" They smiled at one another, and within a few minutes, the rest of the royal party were loading into the limo's and they were quickly escorted into downtown Amsterdam to pick out their decorations. Linda and Billy continued to fire ideas past one another, often confusing one another on their choices, but enjoying themselves nonetheless. After deciding on the streamers, and the icing for the cake (Billy winning the plan with a whipped cream topping. *White represents royalty* was his backup) Linda began the twenty questions game of his life. After a while, Billy looked up from the pile of streamers at Linda.

"What would happen if you told your dad you were dating me? I mean to say, if we WERE dating that is?"

Linda stopped sifting through the decorations and grew quiet. "He would probably make me choose my royal crown, or you."

"Oh," Billy mumbled. "I can see how it would be hard to choose something like that." He looked up at Linda to find her smiling at him.

"When I go to college, graduate, and find a job, I would tell him I pick you."

"I appreciate that Linda. I can't imagine how hard it would be to cut your parents off. I mean, you may try to let go of them, but they won't let go of you. Somewhere down the line, it may get the best of you. But, your father I'm sure loves you very much, and in the end, would respect your decisions no matter what."

Linda took hold of his hand. "Thanks Billy, I appreciate hearing that."

Billy smiled and shrugged her off. "Hey, no problem!"

Linda continued with her questions. "Billy, why don't you have a girlfriend?"

Billy shrugged. "I'm not the type of guy girls normally like to date."

"How do you know?" Asked Linda.

"I've seen all the TV shows, girls wants guys with money, good looks, cars and everything. And well . . . . I have none of that. What about you? What do you want in a guy?"

"Someone like you. A guy who doesn't have to be "perfect" and he likes me for who I am."

Billy nodded. "Someone who likes you for who you are then?"

Linda looked at him warmly. "Exactly."

They stared at each other for what for Billy to be forever. As he looked back at her, he could feel both himself and her slowly pulling towards each other. Their moment snapped off suddenly by the sound of a car door shutting. The limos had returned, and soon, they were escorted back home. Billy and Linda chose a quiet room to set up their decorations and quickly got to work. Linda looked over Billy's choices for the streamers.

"These are really cool Billy," She replied as she stretched them out. "I didn't know you mastered in decorating."

"I have an aunt who was an interior decorator. I sued to work for her for a couple of summers."

Linda smiled coyly. "For a while there, when you were making those suggestions, I thought maybe you were . . . ."

Billy's eyes grew wide. "No! No! I'm not! I'm just a guy with good taste is all."

Linda shrugged, grinning. "Just wondering."

Billy quickly changed subjects. "What the deal with Walter? How long have you known him?"

"For about five years now," Linda answered. "He used to work for a catering company, and often catered for some of my dad's events. At one of the balls, my dad asked who was in charge of it all and Walter introduced himself. My father hired him, and soon Walter found himself as my dad's royal advisor. I've always thought of him more as a mentor than an advisor."

"You look up to him don't you?"

"Yeah, he lets me make my own decisions when my dad isn't around."

"Linda, what if I talked with him about you . . . about us, but told him I'm not royalty, what would he say?"

Linda thought for a moment. "I honestly think he would be ok with it. It would be a shock at first. Why? Do you want to go home? We can tell him if you would want." She looked away from him then and went back to her work.

"Linda, I'm glad you invited me, and I'm not going anywhere. I'm going to finish strong this week, and then maybe we can tell your dad in person who I am. If worst comes to worst, he will probably take my crown away from me and send me home."

"That, or, he would just send you to the dungeons in chains. Ha! Just kidding, but sending you home sounds the more likely response. Whatever the outcome though, I know that I would choose you Billy."

.   .   .   .

Walter entered into the room that belonged to Prince Antonio and Princess Diane. He quickly examined their centerpiece and turned to face the couple. "It's not bad, but I honestly wouldn't put it in the royal ball. Nevertheless, you have both passed the first section, congratulations."

Prince Antonio, pulled back a long strange of dark hair from his face. "Thank you sir."

Walter smiled, bowed, and quickly moved on to the next room. Antonio followed him out.

"Excuse me sir, but may I ask a question?"

Walter turned back to Antonio, his expression blank.

"By chance, is the lady Linda dating anyone presently?"

Walter raised an eyebrow to his question. "No one at the moment no. That's a question you should take to her father. I would honestly think he would approve of you, but it is up to him."

Antonio grinned. "Thank you sir."

Walter nodded quickly and continued back down the hall. Antonio returned to his partner Diane, who was busy with the centerpiece.

"Diane, what do you know about Linda? I really like her."

She shook her head, laughing under her breath. "Keep dreaming. Even if you ask her out, she will probably turn you down."

Antonio was taken aback by her response. "How could she turn ME down?" He responded curtly. "I'm good looking, rich, and soon to be the most powerful man in my country!"

"Well, truth be known Antonio, I think she's in love with Prince William."

The dark haired prince looked at her wide-eyed. William!? That nerdy prince from the Ukraine!? She likes him?"

"Yeah, but a boy like that can be easily brushed aside," she continued. I could seem him most likely stepping aside if you told him you liked her."

Antonio sat down and grew silent. "Perhaps Diane, perhaps. But I need to be sure nonetheless. I need to get some dirt on him. That way, not only is he brushed aside, but blown completely out of this country."

Diane stood behind him. "Forget about Linda. Why don't you date me instead? I am a princess after all and I . . ."

"You may be a princess, but you're not the right match for me Diane. I need someone to match my intellect, looks, and someone that will look great standing next to me. Trust me, Linda is my match."

Diane went back to her decorating. "Keep dreaming moron. You can't just force someone like Linda to be your trophy girlfriend, date, or whatever you want to call her."

"That's why I need you to assist me. I need to you come up with some information about our Prince William."

"What makes you think I would go along with your plan hmm?"

Antonio looked up at her and smiled greedily. "Because you can resist my charm or my good looks; you like it when I take charge."

"You're sick Antonio, do you know that?" Diane sighed heavily under her dress. "What do I have to do?"

. . . .

Walter looked up from Billy and Linda's display, with a bittersweet expression. "You didn't pass the section . . . . but I'm going to put it in the royal ball."

Billy and Linda smiled at one another. Walter bowed slightly and exited the room. The couple headed out of the room towards the royal dining room.

"So when do you think you'll get your letter from the school?" Asked Billy.

Linda shrugged. "Some mail arrived for me today while we were, perhaps I got something back. If I don't get in, I wouldn't have to tell my father, then I would have to go to Oxford which I'm sure I would hate. If I do get in, I would have to tell him. I'm worried that he will be angry and cut me off Billy. I swear, this is a no-win situation we have here."

Billy leaned in and whispered, "Don't give up yet ok?" He winked at her before they entered the dining room. The feast laid out for the Billy and students was extravagant. Years of Thanksgiving dinners had nothing on this one in Billy's eye. As he sat down, he looked across the table to see Antonio glaring back at him. Diane sat down next to him. Antonio looked over at her to see her holding a camera.

"I'm going to get a photo of him."

Antonio leaned in close to her. "How is getting a photo going to help us get any information on him?"

"I can email the photo to my father and he can run a criminal background check on him. That could hopefully get us the information we need. Besides . . . I don't think is who he says he is."

"How do you know that!?" Hissed Antonio.

Diane waved him off. "Princess instincts I guess."

"Well you better take it before starts in on his meal."

"Why Antonio? What did you do?"

He shrugged. "Just put some hot sauce in his gravy before he came to the table. And I put glue on his seat. He's going nowhere."

"You put glue on his seat!? How did you know he would sit there?"

He looked over at Diane. "Prince instincts I guess."

Billy helped himself to a little bit of everything, and as the prince across from him predicted, his mouth soon caught fire from the hot sauce. Billy began to sweat profusely, first downing his glass of water, then moving for the pitcher in front of him. He frantically looked up and down the table as he saw the eyes of his fellow classmates eyeing him suspiciously.

"Excuse me for a moment everyone, but I think . . ."

Billy's eyes grew wide as the glue in his seat caught hold of his pants, causing him to topple over, spilling water all over himself. Laughter filled the room as the other princes and princesses began to laugh hysterically over the sad display. After managing to pry himself away from his seat, Billy excused himself from the room to go clean up.

"Well played sir." Diane said as she sat back down. "I managed to get a photo off before his little "accident". I'll send it to my father, shouldn't be but a couple of days."

"Take all the time you need." Replied Antonio.

.   .   .   .

Linda paced back and forth in her bedroom. Her roommate Jessica watched.

"He's going to be fine Linda. It's not the first time a prince split his pants or was glued to his chair. It was actually quite funny, is it prank day here or something?"

Linda stopped pacing. "I doubt that Jessica. Somebody has it in for William, I think we may have an enemy here."

"Who?" Jessica asked.

"Whoever it is Jess, I think we should warn William."

They quickly shuffled out of the room and across the hall to Billy's room. Linda knocked quietly and entered the room to find Billy and Walter sitting, watching a baseball game on television.

"What game are you watching?" Asked Linda.

"Angels versus Yankees, you're welcome to join us if you'd like?"

Both girls looked at each other and nodded. "I wouldn't want to miss the game." Replied Linda, sitting down next to Jessica. Jessica shifted slightly in her seat, her eyes staying fixed on the game. She pulled a large packet from her hoodie and shoved it towards Linda.

"By the way Linda, this came for you today, sorry I forgot to tell you."

Linda looked down to see the return address clearly labeled "U.S.C." The packet was thick, which could only be a good sign. She remained silent about through the game and enjoyed her company. As they ate pizza and down Diet Pepsi, the game soon came to a close, and Walter ushered the girls out of the room. Outside the room, Linda told Walter she would only be a minute. He bade her goodnight and walked down the hall to his quarters.

She quickly turned around knocked on Billy's door. He answered, already in his pajamas. He looked at her and then to the packet, recognizing it.

"Did you get in!?"

Linda managed a weak smile. "I did, but my dad is not going to be happy about the news."

"We can talk with your dad at the ball Linda. Whether he likes it or not, this is your decision, and you should decide where you want to go. If it means he might cut you off, well . . . so be it. It's your choice, not his."

"You're right, I'm just scared about hurting him. By the way, I'm sorry about what happened at dinner tonight.

Billy looked down at the ground, his face growing red with embarrassment.

"Yeah that, it's alright. I don't know who pulled it, but it doesn't matter, it still doesn't make me want to leave."

"Billy, I'm afraid someone wants to run you off. Please just be careful. In the meantime though, if we catch them, we'll throw them out of the castle."

Billy smiled and nodded. "Sounds like a plan to me. Like I said, don't worry about your dad. Just go, and get some rest. I will see you in the morning ok?"

"All right Billy, thanks again for . . . everything. Goodnight."

"Linda, one last thing. Am I going to make it through all of this?"

A light shown in Linda's eyes as she looked back at him. She smiled. "Without a doubt."

Billy nodded and closed the door. The look of her smile hung in his mind as he climbed into bed. He felt warmer than ever, and even in the dark, he could see himself smiling. *I'm going to make it here. If I don't, I'll die trying.*

. . . .

The second day of Princess School continued to swing in Billy and Linda's favor. Day two marked the section, which involved baking that both Billy and Linda won in Walter's eyes. Their cake was to be added to the ball and the rest of the day went off without any accidents or incidents from Antonio. On the third day, the couples were judged on their invitations, which was won yet again by Billy and Linda.

The fourth day was a bit more of a challenge for them both when trying to decide on proper clothing to wear to the ball. Billy continued to come up with ideas, but Linda remained a bit skeptical on some of his choices. After making a quick glance over Antonio and Diane's ideas, he shook his head, not fully convinced.

"And what do our star students have in store for me today I wonder?" Walter asked.

Billy explained to Walter that the ball should be in casual wear. If it was to mark the birthday of princess Linda, it should reflect more her choices on what she would like. He suggest casual wear, from a nice casual gown or shirts and slacks, to jeans and a t-shirt if need be. Walter smiled over his clipboard and nodded. "Top marks yet again William."

Later in the day, Linda and Billy were busy planning what form of entertainment could best serve the guests. Billy suggested that a band should perform, but went even further by suggesting The Rolling Stones. The cards favored his choice as Walter yet again marked Billy and Linda down for the winners of the day. As the sunrise marked the fifth and last day of the school, the students were talking nervously in the hall about their thoughts on who would win the competition. Soon enough, Walter entered the room and stood before them all.

"Well students, this is the last day of Princess School. The princess ball graduation will take place during the royal ball itself, marking Princess Linda's birthday. Thank you all again for your hard work, you will make excellent dignitaries to your country. The winners are as follows: Princess Jessica of Romania and our valedictorian prince is Prince William of the Ukraine. May we give these two a hand please?"

A light splutter of clapping echoed in the room as the students looked to one another, some pleased, others clearly disappointed.

"Yes yes, well done to you all," continued Walter. "It will be up to the valedictorians to decide which of your ideas to use in the ball. Pitch them your ideas if you would like, tomorrow we will be decorating for the ball itself, which is to be held on Saturday. You can invite whomever you would like, but always remember to treat one another with the utmost respect. Again, thank you all, and congratulations to our winners."

They began to make their way back to their rooms. Billy escorted Linda back to her room, both smiling as they walked.

Antonio continued to stare coldly at the couple as they passed. He looked over to see Diane standing next to him.

"I'm not going to let some loser prince like William steal Linda from me Diane."

"I don't know, I think he's kind of a nice guy actually Antonio."

The prince grabbed her arm and squeezed it. "Trust me—no member of royalty is ever that nice. I want to make sure he doesn't set foot in that ball."

"Well, if it will make you feel any better, I received an email back from my dad."

Antonio spun to meet her eyes. "Well? What of it?"

"I don't think Prince William is who he says he is. Apparently from the report, he has no link to royalty. His name is William Malcolm to be certain, but he's a senior Anaheim High School in California of the United States. He graduated two weeks ago, his parents are middle class, and he has a little sister by the name of Erica. He's a commoner Antonio. Should we inform Linda's father?"

Antonio grinned maliciously. "I'll handle this Diane."

. . . .

Walter entered the hallway to find Billy already surrounded by the princesses asking him for his advice. He agreed to some of the their ideas, often complimenting them and allowing their ideas to be on display at the ball.

"Excuse me William, but I have contacted the Rolling Stones manager and it looks like they are on tour at the moment. Do you have any other ideas? Billy's smile stretched across his face as he came up a solution.

"May I use your phone Walter? I need to make a call. I have a friend named Jimmy that's in a band, I could call to see if he could make it."

"Certainly sir, follow me." Walter led him down another corridor to his office. Billy made the call back home and instructed Jimmy of where to be and when. It took some convincing (Jimmy knew Billy was always out to one-up him on jokes) but finally, Jimmy agreed to meet Billy's supposed jet at the airport. Billy also called his parents reminding them to meet at the same time and place as Jimmy for a surprise they would not soon forget. He hung up the phone and looked at Walter sitting across the table from him.

"We're all set Walter. The entertainment factor is taken care of, and we are good to go with the ball."

Walter smiled from across the table. "I forgot to mention sir, but I have a friend of mine that owns a record company. It's been a long while since I've last seen him so I extended the invitation to him as well. Would you mind at all?"

"Not at all Walter, the more the merrier."

"Very good sir. And thank you sir."

Billy nodded. "By the way, if you're up for it tonight, there's another game on TV if you would care to watch?"

"I would like that very much William. Shall I inform Princess Linda and Jessica as well?"

"Definitely. Pizza again?"

Walter grinned. "Definitely sir."

They left the office and walked back to the rooms. Walter took quick leave of Billy to tell the girls leaving him alone. Billy heard shuffling behind him and turned to see Antonio and Diane coming up behind him.

"Hey guys, if you're wanting to pitch some more ideas for the ball, I'm sorry, but they've been filled."

"I'm not here to pitch ideas William," replied the prince. "There is something we need to talk with you about."

"What is it?"

"Come by my room." The three of them entered Antonio's room where they all stood staring at one another.

"You care to tell me what this is about then?"

Antonio went to his desk and handed Billy a piece of paper. Billy could feel his stomach drop as he read his personal information.

"I've got to say William, you sure know your way around this school. I've always wanted to ask a royal member of the Ukraine family how he talks with an American accent? But more so, how they act like Americans, talk and dress like them, and all pull off that . . . middle class style of theirs."

"Just lucky I guess Antonio." Mumbled Billy.

"I think you should take a look a good look at that paper *your highness*," Replied Diane. "Turns out, you're not royalty at all. Your dad is an engineer, and your mom is a homemaker. All the way from Anaheim, California. Sound about right?"

Antonio continued. "Looks like the cats out of the bag huh Billy boy? What I wanted to ask you was what an American commoner such as yourself is doing here in Gunther's court trying to imitate a royal prince?"

"I was invited here by mistake," replied Billy. "I got the message in the mail and I thought it was a practical prank from one of my friends back home. I went along with it until I arrived here and realized it wasn't. I was going to tell Walter, but I changed my mind. The school wasn't so bad after all."

"But Billy, *how* did you get the invitation sent to you?" Asked Diane. "Do you realize how much trouble you are going to be in with Linda's father?"

Billy looked up then from the paper. "Diane, I knew the risk when I first came here, but I wanted to take a chance."

"You didn't answer her question," replied Antonio. "*How* did you get invited to the school in the first place?"

Billy threw the paper down, glaring back at Antonio. "Look, I'm not going to tell you. If you want to tell Walter or the king then be my guest."

"I could tell the king sure. But I already have a pretty good idea who sent you the letter." Antonio took a minute and eyed Billy up and down. "Do you actually think you would stand a chance with a beautiful princess like Linda when I'm here? Linda would never fall for a nerdy commoner like you."

Billy shrugged. "You never know."

"Why do you say that?" Asked Diane.

"Because I've been her computer pen pal for some time now. Of all the guys her father would try to hook her up with or, *princes* that may want her, she wants to date *me*. A person who listens to her and sees her for who she really is. Name one time you ever listened to her or even saw the real *her*."

Antonio put ups his hands. "You got me. I'm not interested in her personality or her dreams and hopes. I'm interested in her beauty and background. Having her at my side would put on quite the appearance in my country."

"Then you're wanting to date her for all the wrong reasons." Replied Billy.

"We have a proposition for you," interjected Diane. "We want you to tell Walter that you are leaving Amsterdam tomorrow and that something came up back home. Never come back here again, and you will also put in a good word for Antonio before you leave."

Billy's mouth hung open slightly at Diane's words.

"Forget it."

"I have a better one for you." Replied Antonio. "You stay here for the rest of the week, decorate, and make all the plans you want for the ball. At the end, you step aside and help me secure a place next to Linda, put in a good word and all that, and forfeit your position to me."

Billy shook his head. "And if I refuse?"

"Then I send the printed information to Linda's father. I'm sure you would spend a bit of time in a locked cell for impersonating royalty."

Billy's heart dropped from his stomach and out of existence. The thoughts he had of Linda and him together were slowly melting away, and all that was left was now what lay before him.

"Fine, I'll do it."

Antonio smiled at his victory. "I knew you'd see it my way, now run along and get to it."

The walk back to his room seemed to take Billy forever. He felt like he had slipped back into his dream state again, where reality now like a dream, and he was lost somewhere on a long road in between. He started to turn doorknob to his room when he heard the door to Linda's room open.

"Billy, where have you been? The game has already started!" Billy turned to face her. Her excited expression as she looked in Billy's eyes. "What's wrong?"

"Can we talk Linda?"

She closed the door softly behind her. "Sure, but before you start, there's something I have to tell you. I . . . I like you Billy. I mean to say, I REALLY like you."

"You do?" Asked Billy.

"That's kind of an understatement really. Honestly, I think I'm in love with you Billy."

Billy looked at the floor. "How? How can you love me? You're a beautiful princess and I'm a total geek."

He felt her hand touch his face as she brought his gaze back to meet hers. Her smile warmed him, and he could feel his old self returning a little.

"Billy, I don't care about any of it. About looks, money, fame. I care about *you;* I like you for who you are, and not what you can be by me."

"Well, since we're being truthful here Linda, I should tell you that I'm in love with you too. But I don't think we can see each other because I'm not exactly the guy you're looking for a prince. I think I'm going to tell Walter the truth. I'm sorry."

Billy looked down again for a moment as he saw tears forming in Linda's eyes. He could see her brush them away from her cheeks and breathe heavily as they continued to stand in the hall.

"What is going on Billy? I love you. There is something going on that you're not telling me. It's not like you to back down like this, unless . . ."

Billy looked back at Linda, surprised.

"Unless someone is trying to blackmail you to leave."

"How do you know that!?"

"I don't. You just told me. Besides, you're not the first person that somebody tried to scare off. I know it's not my father," she paused for a moment thinking. "It has to be Antonio."

"You know that guy?" Asked Billy.

"He asked me out a few times at past conventions. I always turned him down; he's such an arrogant jerk. I know that he doesn't see me for who I am, he just wants a trophy. Someone to make *him* look good."

"I'm sorry Linda."

"Why would you try to break up with me Billy?"

"Well . . . let's just say, he found out about me. Diane was in on it too. She took a picture of me this past week after the dinner fiasco and sent the info to her dad. They ran a background check on me. They plan to tell your father and Walter."

Linda began to pace in front of Billy. "I'm not going to see myself with that guy. Look Billy, we may not see each other after this because with the plan I have in mind, we're going to do something that could banish you from this country."

"Sounds great." Replied Billy. Linda waved him off.

"Yeah, BUT, if we play our cards right, I think it's time we let Antonio have a taste of his own medicine."

"How Linda?"

"WE'RE going to tell my father the truth before Antonio."

"Excuse me?"

Linda grabbed Billy by the arm and they sprinted down the hall. "Don't worry Billy, I have a plan."

Billy rolled his eyes. *I hate it when you say that*, he thought to himself.

· · · ·

They found Walter and Linda's father, King Gunther in the throne room. Both men's eyes were locked over a chessboard, calculating the other's move. Walter stood as the couple approached; the king peered up from the board and smiled at his daughter.

"Linda! Hi honey, what's on your mind this evening?"

"Father, I want you to meet Prince William of the Ukraine."

The king stood and Billy bowed slightly, not knowing the proper protocol. "Your Majesty."

"Please, no need for that William. Walter tells me you had top marks throughout the week, congratulations."

"Thank you, I appreciate your kind words your highness. However, there is something that Linda and I need to talk with you both about."

Judging from the looks on their faces, Gunther's face changed from happy to concern. He once again began twirling his beard in his fingers. Billy stepped forward.

"There is no Prince William of the Ukraine."

Walter and the king exchanged quick glances. "Excuse me!? What are you talking about William?" Asked Gunther.

"My name is Billy," he looked over at Walter. "Walter, I'm from Anaheim, California. I grew up in a middle class family. Linda and I have been pen pals for some time now; she invited me to attend this Princess School so we could get to know one another."

Linda stepped up next to Billy. "It's true father, I love Billy. I know you don't approve, but it's the only way I could meet him. I don't . . . I *can't* lose him."

The king collapsed back in his seat while Walter continued to stand, shocked and bewildered at the news. Linda leaned in close to Billy. "This is going to be a long day." Billy nodded whispering back, "Tell me about it."

. . . .

The following morning, the students of Princess School began their decorating for the ball. Billy remained in charge and directed the princes and princesses to their jobs. While the others were busy printing invitations, setting streamers, and planning out the different array of foods, Billy managed to signal Antonio with a thumbs up that everything was in order. He nodded curtly and when back to work.

They continued to work into the afternoon and once everything was in its place, they returned to their rooms to get ready for the evening. Walter helped Billy picked out a good relaxing outfit for the ball. Billy looked over his shoulder as Walter sized him up with a sport jacket.

"How is the king doing with Linda's news about wanting to go to U.S.C.?"

Walter remained silent for a moment, continuing with his work. "It's a lot to take in, in such a short span of time, but I'm sure he'll be ok."

"Do you think he'll be ok with me dating his daughter after hearing the truth about me?"

"You best give him some time on that one Billy. But for this plan of yours, I think we're all set."

He finished and put the jacket on Billy. Billy admired himself in the mirror for a moment, smiling only slightly. "I guess we better get ready then."

"One more thing Billy. I meant what I said earlier in the week. You're going to do amazing things out there, after graduation. I just hope someday you make your country proud."

Billy smiled. "That's the plan."

Walter escorted Billy to the main hall where a sea of people was there to greet him. He looked to the stage to see his friend Jimmy and his band plucking away at a slow ballad, Jimmy all the while looking shocked, trying to muddle his way through the song. *I got you Jimmy, at long last.* Billy smiled as he waved to his friend. Walter leaned in close to Billy.

"Son, above all else, just be yourself with Linda. Don't try to be something you're not."

Billy turned and took Walter's hand and shook.

"Thanks for everything Walter. You're a true friend."

"I appreciate that William, truly. I best go wait for the king, good luck kid."

Seconds later, Billy felt another hand on him. He turned to see Antonio's dark eyes staring back at him. "So did you do it? You got me with her?"

"Yeah Antonio. I told her everything. She was ecstatic when I told her you liked her. Sad thing is, she was just using me to make you jealous. You were right; I'm no prince, just a commoner. So go ahead and have your laugh when her father kicks me out."

"How does that sit with you Billy boy?"

"It doesn't matter. I know you want me out of here because I'm a threat standing in the way of Linda. I beg you though, don't tell her father. I really like this school."

"Ahh, that just doesn't sit right with my Billy. Who would I be if I didn't see this all the way through? Threat or no, you're still here, and still in my way which I find annoying. Will I tell her father? Most likely, just figured I would give you a head's up beforehand. I'm a generous guy when I need to be."

"Yeah, a regular saint you are."

At the far end of the court, the ladies were entering into the room. The crowd parted as Linda made her way towards Billy. Antonio clapped him on the shoulder again.

"Enjoy your one and only dance with her Billy boy, you'll never get another chance at anything so good in your life."

Linda's dress glided around her like a silk cloud. She was absolutely radiant in her dress. Billy concluded that it was definitely for the best that Linda changed the attire at the last minute. Never had he seen her or any other girl look so beautiful. He blinked only once, and before he knew it, she was standing in front of him.

"Well are you just going to stand there and drool or we have a dance together?"

Billy continued to stand and stare, dumbstruck by her appearance. She smiled and rolled her eyes as she took hold of his hand dragged him to the dance floor. Billy walked over to greet his friend Jimmy for a quick moment to request a song and quickly rushed back to her. The song began, and soon Jimmy's voice rang out over the crowd with the song *I'll Be* by Edwin McCain.

While they danced, Antonio stood brooding the corner and Diane made her way over to him.

"Where is Linda's father?" She asked.

He nodded to the far end of the room. She could see the king in the kitchen preparing something for the evening, possibly a late night snack.

"Do you have the file?" He snapped at her.

"I have it right here." She pointed to her purse. He snatched it out of her hand and pulled the file from the bag.

"It's time to end this so I can get on with this stupid evening and be crowned!" She watched him as he strode across the room and up to King Gunther. She watched as he showed him the information and the two exchanged words. She walked a bit closer to hear their conversation.

"Are you sure of this Antonio?"

"Beyond any doubt your Majesty."

The king called for Walter. "Walter! Get Lumiere up here."

"The captain of the guards sir? I haven't seen him."

The king's face grew red as he glared at Walter. "He's guarding the front door. Get him over here now!"

"At once sir!"

While the guards made their way through the crowd to surround the dancing couple, both Linda and Billy remained focused on one another. They continued their dance a few moments longer, but were soon cut short when Lumiere stepped in between them. The king ordered the band to cease playing, and soon, all was silent in the room.

"Father, what is going on?" Linda demanded.

"Your *Prince* William . . . is not who he says he is. He is a commoner from the United States!" He turned to Billy. "What have you to say in your defense young sir!?"

Billy looked around the room, his face a mix of both shock and embarrassment. "I'm really me sire, and I truly love your daughter. We are pen pals, and when she told me about this Princess School, I wanted to come. So . . . I . . . I lied. I lied my way in and used up my life savings to pay for my ticket and my ride here. I am truly sorry to have deceived you your Majesty. And everyone here."

Gunther turned to Linda. "I wouldn't have found this information out if it hadn't been for Antonio. He is the one who is in love with you; he knew he didn't trust this fake prince from the start."

Antonio stepped in behind the king. "I knew that guy was a threat when I first saw him. I knew he was trying to steal my girl."

Linda turned on her heel. "I'm NOT your girl, you jerk! I'm my own person. Billy may have lied his way in here, but one thing I can tell is that Billy is a better man than you will EVER be! Father, please don't do this!"

Gunther shook his head. "I'm sorry my dear, but he lied and this man is a commoner. Antonio will be rewarded for his part."

Linda looked at him shocked. "His part of what?"

"Antonio will be betrothed to you, and he will be valedictorian of the Princess School."

"Dad you can't do this!"

Gunther turned back to Billy. "William Malcolm, under the laws of the Netherlands, you will be banished from this country and my daughter. You will be removed from this school and forfeit your position. Is that understood?"

Billy nodded in dismay. "Yes, your highness."

The king put a hand on Billy's shoulder. "You understand the consequences of your actions?" Again, Billy nodded. He could feel himself growing smaller and smaller by the minute. He just wanted to be back home where his normal life waited for him. He looked up as the king beckoned for his guards. He cast a side-glance at Antonio, who grinned from ear to ear. He continued to do so for a short moment even after the guards brushed past Billy and took hold of Antonio. Soon enough, the grin on his face was replaced with utter confusion.

"Your Majesty, what's going on here!?"

"Prince Antonio, consider yourself expelled from Princess School. You tried to break my daughter's relationship with this young man, my number one pupil of the school."

"But . . . I . . ."

"Don't understand?" Billy asked, as he stepped forward. "I'll sum it up. Linda and I decided to tell the king ourselves of your little plan and the truth behind myself. Everyone already knows I'm a commoner," He nodded towards the girl standing next to Antonio. "Diane told them, she was in on it too."

Diane looked over at the captive prince. "I knew you hated Billy, since he first came here, and I knew you were in love with Linda "Princess Instincts" remember? Do you think I was going to let her date an arrogant jerk like you? So, I informed her myself and got you in on this little scam. She told Billy, and he, the king. And so it goes."

"I thought they would throw me out at first," continued Billy. "But after I told them the truth, they were cool with it. More than anything, they just wanted Linda happy."

The king cleared his throat. "Antonio, you are to be banished from my country and my daughter. Unless, of course, you apologize to Billy."

Antonio looked frantic. "Apologize to THAT commoner!? Forget it! I'd rather jump in the moat than apologize to that geek!"

King Gunther waved his comment off. "So be it. Guards, remove him from this castle and put him on the first flight back to his country. Send a report to his parents. I dread the thought of King Alexander when he reads this news."

The guards pulled the prince kicking and screaming from the room, and soon the room was left with the commotion of the guests. Billy took hands with the king.

"Sire, thank you for everything."

"Good grip you have there son. Anything for my daughter, and speaking of . . ." He turned to face his daughter. "I want you to be happy, if that means going to U.S.C. will make you so, then I'm on board."

Linda grabbed her father within a flash and held him close, tears streaming down her face. "Thank you father."

Amongst the crowd, Billy managed to find Jimmy and gave him a quick hug.

"Thanks Jimmy."

"Hey! No problemo! I owe you one man. Thanks to you, I have a record deal. Mr. Rayne over there is from *Jive Records* and he just signed me for a five-year recording contract! I really owe you one Billy."

"No problemo." Replied Billy.

A few moments later, the procession commenced and the king, along with Walter, announced the winners of Princess School. As the procession ended however, the king gave one final announcement.

"Ladies and gentleman, for our valedictorian of this Princess School, I give you Prince William Malcolm of Anaheim."

Billy blinked once. "Wait, what!?"

"Kneel kid!" Walter hissed under his breath and winked.

Billy kneeled as a sword was brought over his left shoulder.

"William Malcolm, you're going to do amazing things one day," proclaimed the king. "Not just from this school, but out there in the real world with my daughter. I hope you and my daughter will continue to make me proud."

Billy looked up over the sword. "I will your highness."

King Gunther finished the ceremony and bade Billy to rise.

"Arise Honorary Prince William of the Netherlands."

A cheer rose from the crowd as he stood, followed with a cascade of applause. The king leaned in close. "You may have the first dance with my daughter."

"King Gunther, thank you sire."

The king waves him off once more. "No need for that, call me Gunther."

Billy smiled and took Linda's hand in his. The dancing proceeded and soon the young couple were lost within their dreams of one another. With Jimmy's voice playing softly over the speakers, and no other dramas or truths to be told, the young couple picked up where they left off on the first day of Princess School, leaned towards one another, and kissed.

. . . .

That kiss continued to play its part in the months ahead, and soon enough, both Billy and Linda found themselves kissing on the front steps of the Communication/Arts building at U.S.C. They broke off for a moment to grab some air and look at their schedules.

"What's your first class your highness?" Asked Linda.

"I think it's filmmaking."

Linda managed to pull of a fake look of shock on her face. "What a coincidence! Mine too!"

Billy smiled. "It's a good thing we're both film majors now."

"You're right. Come on, we don't want to miss class, and we DEFINITELY don't want to disappoint my father."

Billy laughed under his breath. "No, we definitely don't want that! Let's go your highness."

They bowed to one another. "As you will my lord." Said Linda.

A warm wind blew around the young royal couple as they found one another back in the other's arms again. The steps up the building were only the first steps towards the rest of the their lives. And they lived happily ever after.

The End